NURSERY

PROJECT

Susan Laughs

Jeanne Willis and Tony Ross

A

Andersen Press • London

Susan laughs,

Susan sings,

Susan flies,

Susan swings.

Susan's good, Susan's bad,

Susan's happy, Susan's sad.

Susan dances,

Susan rides,

Susan swims,

Susan hides.

Susan's shy,   Susan's loud,

Susan's angry,   Susan's proud.

Susan splashes,

Susan spins,

Susan waves,

Susan grins.

Susan's right,   Susan's wrong,

Susan's weak,   Susan's strong.

Susan trots,

Susan rows,

Susan paints,

Susan throws.

Susan feels, Susan fears,

Susan hugs, Susan hears.

That is Susan
through and through –
just like me, just like you.

First published in Great Britain in 1999 by Andersen Press Ltd., 20 Vauxhall Bridge Road, London SW1V 2SA.
Published in Australia by Random House Australia Pty., 20 Alfred Street, Milsons Point, Sydney, NSW 2061.
All rights reserved. Colour separated in Switzerland by Photolitho AG, Zurich.
Printed and bound in Italy by Grafiche AZ, Verona.

10   9   8   7   6   5   4   3   2   1

British Library Cataloguing in Publication Data available.

ISBN 0 86264 896 3

This book has been printed on acid-free paper